CRANBERRY CHRISTMAS

Wende and Harry Devlin

PARENTS' MAGAZINE PRESS · NEW YORK

JE

Library of Congress Cataloging in Publication Data

Devlin, Wende.
  Cranberry Christmas.
  SUMMARY: Mr. Whiskers faces a gloomy Christmas
until Maggie and her grandmother help him straighten
out his house and find the deed to the nearby pond.
  [1. Christmas stories] I. Devlin, Harry, joint
author. II. Title.
PZ7.D499Cr   [E]   76-2524
ISBN 0-8193-0844-7   ISBN 0-8193-0845-5 lib. bdg.

c.4

for Elizabeth Wende

CHRISTMAS was coming! Snow was on the cranberry bog,
the smell of pine in the wind, and the fresh water pond
frozen smooth.
Mr. Whiskers, looking out from his kitchen window,
was deep in gloom.

Christmas was only three days away and his pond should have
been filled with skaters—skaters in bright sweaters, laughing,
with their scarves flying in the wind. And he should have
been there teaching them all to twirl and do figure eights.

But old Cyrus Grape had changed all that. He had moved next door to Mr. Whiskers, into the stone house on the rise, and claimed that the pond was on his land. Cyrus didn't like children. Whenever he saw them on the pond, he would hop on his sled and slide bumpity-bump down the hill.

"Scat! Off my pond or I'll have the sheriff after you!" Cyrus
would shout as he shook his cane and chased the skaters
to the snowy banks.
"It's my pond, you old scoundrel! Mine!" Mr. Whiskers would
boom back.

But when the old sea captain searched through the attic, the desk, and the cellar of his little gray cottage, he could find nothing to prove that he owned the pond. He began to wonder if he *did* own the pond.

Mr. Whiskers brooded.
Cyrus Grape cackled.
And the little children sadly
hung up their skates.

Today there were new troubles for Mr. Whiskers. A letter
from his persnickity sister Sarah in the city announced that
she was coming for Christmas. And after the holidays she
expected him to come back to the city to live with her.
"You can't take care of yourself. Your house looks like
a shipwreck and your money box is always empty," she scolded
in her letter.
Mr. Whiskers frowned. He liked the way he took care of himself.
In the summer, he clammed and felt the water and sand on his
bare feet. In the winter, he ice-skated with the children
all around him like a school of fish.

To think of leaving Cranberryport! The idea of living in
the city with Sarah and her striped cat made Mr. Whiskers
furious! Fuming, he took his troubles to Maggie and Grandmother
who lived in a farmhouse on the other side of the dunes.
"Suffering codfish! What can I do?" He waved his letter
in their kitchen.

When Grandmother heard Mr. Whiskers' news, she held her head.
A guest at Mr. Whiskers' jumbled house!
"You haven't borrowed my broom since summer," she chided.
"I sweep in the spring," said Mr. Whiskers, looking at the
ceiling. Grandmother shook her head.
She and Maggie didn't waste time. Mr. Whiskers certainly
needed help. In a few minutes, loaded with Grandmother's
soap and polish and bristling with brooms and brushes, all
three took the path to Mr. Whiskers' house, over the dunes
on the ocean side.

They went to work.
How they worked!
Maggie washed the windows.
Mr. Whiskers scrubbed the floor.
Grandmother dusted and gave orders.
"What's this behind the couch?"
"Lobster pots," Mr. Whiskers answered.
"What's this in the bathtub?"
"My shell collection," growled Mr. Whiskers.
"Out with them all," ordered Grandmother.

Mr. Whiskers grumbled about persnickity sisters and certain grandmothers, but he did as he was told.

It was at the end of the second day of helping Mr. Whiskers that the accident happened. Maggie had trimmed the pine tree and baked her favorite cranberry cookies. She had just put the last pan away when she heard a loud crash in the pantry. Suddenly, there were Mr. Whiskers' feet sticking right through the ceiling.

Maggie raced upstairs.

Poor Mr. Whiskers! With help from Maggie, he groaned and pulled himself up. It was then that Maggie spied the dusty black and gold box between the floor and ceiling.

Carefully, they pulled it out into the light.

"A treasure, Mr. Whiskers," said Maggie with shining eyes.

"Not in my house," sighed Mr. Whiskers as he carried the box downstairs.

He was right. It was filled with photographs and dusty old papers.

But long after Maggie left, Mr. Whiskers was still studying the papers in the orange light of afternoon. He opened the last stiff parchment and began to smile. Now he chuckled. Then he slapped his knee and shouted, "Suffering codfish!"

Christmas Eve brought a light snow to Cranberryport and
the smell of the sea was in the air.

Mr. Whiskers' sister, Sarah—a round, brown-eyed woman
with a flowered bag—arrived from the train station in
Cranberryport's only taxicab.

Mr. Whiskers hugged her and introduced Sarah all around.
She turned and stared at the cottage.

"How clean your windows are, Brother!"
"I love to shine the blinking things," he boomed.
Grandmother sniffed and Maggie laughed.

But when Sarah went inside the cottage, she could scarcely believe her eyes. She had never seen such a beautiful sight.

The wooden table was polished and set with holly and red candles.

And the Christmas tree! It was a celebration of
sea shells. There had been no money for ornaments,
so Maggie and Mr. Whiskers had painted the shell
collection. It glistened with silver and gold.
There were chains of snail shells, silver clam shells,
and a golden starfish at the top.
Sarah clapped her hands. "Brother, you're a
wonder!"
Mr. Whiskers smiled behind his whiskers.

The night was a triumph—from the supper of clam chowder, Grandmother's famous bread, hot spiced cider, and Maggie's cranberry cookies to the singing of carols around the old piano.

Mr. Whiskers pretended to cover his ears when Grandmother trilled on the high notes.

And there were gifts from the old sea captain—a seaworn
bottle, blue as a sapphire, for Grandmother, a giant pink
shell for Maggie, and a small ivory box for Sarah. Sarah
dipped into her flowered bag and presented her brother with
a new red knitted scarf and mittens.

It was midnight. As Maggie left, Mr. Whiskers whispered into her ear that the children of Cranberryport should be at the pond at noon tomorrow. He winked in a most mysterious way.

Christmas afternoon was cold and bright. Mr. Whiskers
darted among the skaters and had just stopped to catch his
breath, when he heard the voice of Cyrus Grape.
"Arrest them all, Sheriff!"

Behind Cyrus stood a tall man with a broad-brimmed hat.
There were screams as the skaters fled in every direction.
All except Mr. Whiskers.
Mr. Whiskers pretended he hadn't heard a thing. He skated,
he whirled, and then he stretched his arms and glided like
a great black-whiskered bird.

Mr. Grape's face grew red.

"Off to jail with you," Cyrus screeched, pulling the sheriff after Mr. Whiskers.

"I'm skating on my own pond, you old fraud!" cried Mr. Whiskers, turning and slowing down until he faced Cyrus Grape. Slowly, triumphantly, he reached into the pocket of his brass-buttoned coat and drew out a yellowed, red-sealed paper and waved it under Cyrus Grape's long nose. He handed it to the sheriff.

The sheriff studied it carefully and looked at Mr. Grape.
"This paper proves that the pond belongs to Mr. Whiskers,"
he said. "You, sir, are trespassing on Mr. Whiskers' pond."
Cyrus Grape turned a deeper red and roared with rage. He
wound his muffler around his face and started up the rise to
his house, pulling his sled behind him.

Mr. Whiskers turned to the children and raised his hand for silence.

"My pond is yours—to skate on whenever you like. Merry Christmas to everyone."

The crowd cheered.

Sarah whispered to him, "My goodness, you certainly can take care of yourself, and all of Cranberryport, too!"

Mr. Whiskers offered his arm to Maggie for a turn on the ice.
They skated off joyfully.

"I'm a wonder," he said to Maggie. And even the whiskers couldn't hide the smile on Mr. Whiskers' face.